MR. MEN
on the Farm
Roger Hargreaves

Original concept by
Roger Hargreaves

Written and illustrated by
Adam Hargreaves

Hello, my name is Walter. Can you spot me in this book?

Mr Silly was very excited. He had just bought a farm.

He had always wanted to be a farmer, Farmer Silly.

And on his farm, he had some cows and sheep and pigs and a duck pond and chickens and an orchard and lots and lots of fields.

The only problem was that Mr Silly had no idea how to be a farmer. Not a clue.

He was so clueless that on his first day he fed cornflakes to the cows.

Cornflakes!

Have you ever heard of anything quite so daft?

And there was more.

He put the pig in the hen house and it got stuck.

He filled the duck pond with custard and the ducks all flew away.

He trained the farm cat to herd the sheep.

A sheepcat!

What nonsense.

All the sheep escaped.

And he trained the sheepdog to collect the eggs.

Which was possibly an even worse idea.

Mr Silly trying to plough his own field was definitely an even worse idea!

Finally, he picked the apples in the orchard with a saw.

By the end of his first week on the farm, everything had gone wrong.

And because everything had gone wrong, there were no apples or sausages for Little Miss Dotty's apple and sausage cake.

There was no milk to go on Mr Greedy's daily packet of cornflakes.

In fact there were no cornflakes because Mr Silly had fed them all to the cows!

And there were no eggs for Mr Strong's breakfast.

Mr Strong decided to investigate and walked up to the farm from town, which took rather longer than normal because he was feeling a bit weak without his usual eggy breakfast.

You might say he was eggshausted!

And at the top of the hill at the farm gate he found Mr Silly, or rather Farmer Silly, admiring his acres and looking as pleased as punch.

"Well, that explains everything," sighed Mr Strong, who set about putting everything straight.

He began by collecting some eggs for his breakfast.

A lot of eggs for a big, Mr Strong breakfast.

Then, once he had regained his strength, he put the pig back in its pigsty.

He arranged for Mr Fussy to replough the field in beautiful straight furrows.

He fed hay to the cows.

He asked Little Miss Neat to replant the apple trees in the orchard in nice neat rows.

And he carried all the sheep back to their paddock.

Then he organised for Mr Greedy to empty the custard from the duck pond.

Everything was just how it should be.

Until he heard a loud cry of "OUT!" come from the other side of the hedge.

Mr Strong peered round the hedge and there was Mr Silly…

... playing tennis with the pig!